DRUMHELLER DINOSAUR DANCE

Written by
Robert Heidbreder

Illustrated by
Bill Slavin and
Esperança Melo

Kids Can Press

Drumheller dinosaurs lie around,
bones buried deep in ancient ground.

Dry bones rest in dusty sleep – skulls, claws,

Drumheller dinosaurs make no

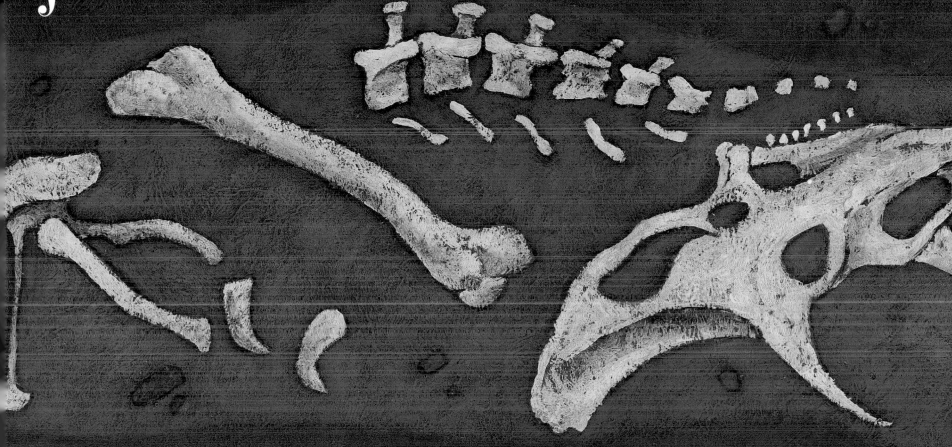

jaws down dinosaur deep.

noise. All day they're as silent as dinosaur toys.

But when the moon rises in the sky,
Drumheller dinosaurs transmogrify.

They stir their bones from secret cracks
and assemble themselves —
fronts, sides and backs.

Drumheller dinosaurs rise up tall.
Across the Badlands they skeleton-crawl.

They creep to a spot that they all know.
They band together, ROAR

They grab buried drums and begin a beat. They

BOOMITY-BOOM   RATTELY-CLACK

rattle, clack, stomp on dinosaur feet.

THUMPITY-THUMP WHICKETY-WHACK

Cymbals crash, stone castanets snap.
They dance back to life with a clickity-clap.

They tango, fandango and break-dance with ease. They whirl on

BOOMITY-BOOM RATTELY-CLACK

their tails and twirl on their knees.

THUMPITY-THUMP
WHICKETY-WHACK

With wild tambourines they shimmy and shake.
They rock and they roll – it's a dino earthquake!

BOOMITY-BOOM RATTELY-CLACK

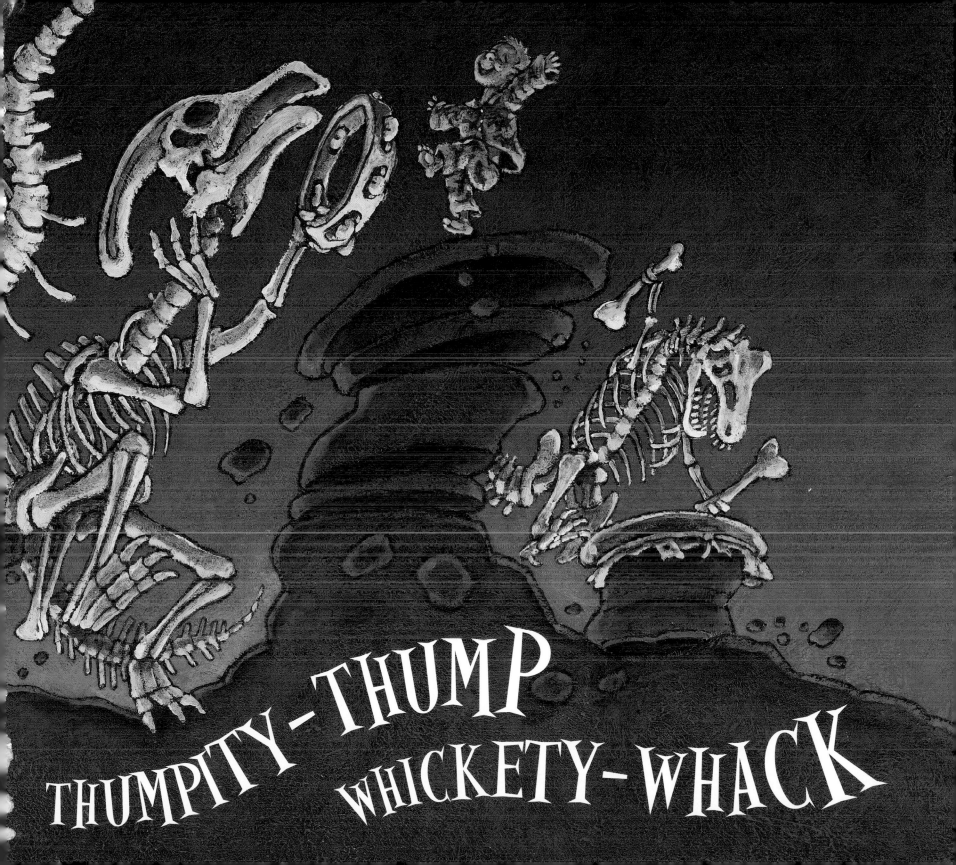

THUMPITY-THUMP
WHICKETY-WHACK

The thunderous beat rolls into town.
Sleep is disturbed for miles around.

"A terrible storm!"
the grown-ups shout.
But the kids all know that the dinos are out.

The dinosaurs' party is loud and long,

BOOMITY-BOOM RATTELY-CLACK

with drumming and dancing and Drumheller song:

THUMPITY-THUMP WHICKETY-WHACK

The kids go to sleep to the dinosaur beat. They bob their heads and tip-tap their feet.

They dance in their dreams
with wiggles and jiggles,
smiles on their faces and mouths full of giggles.

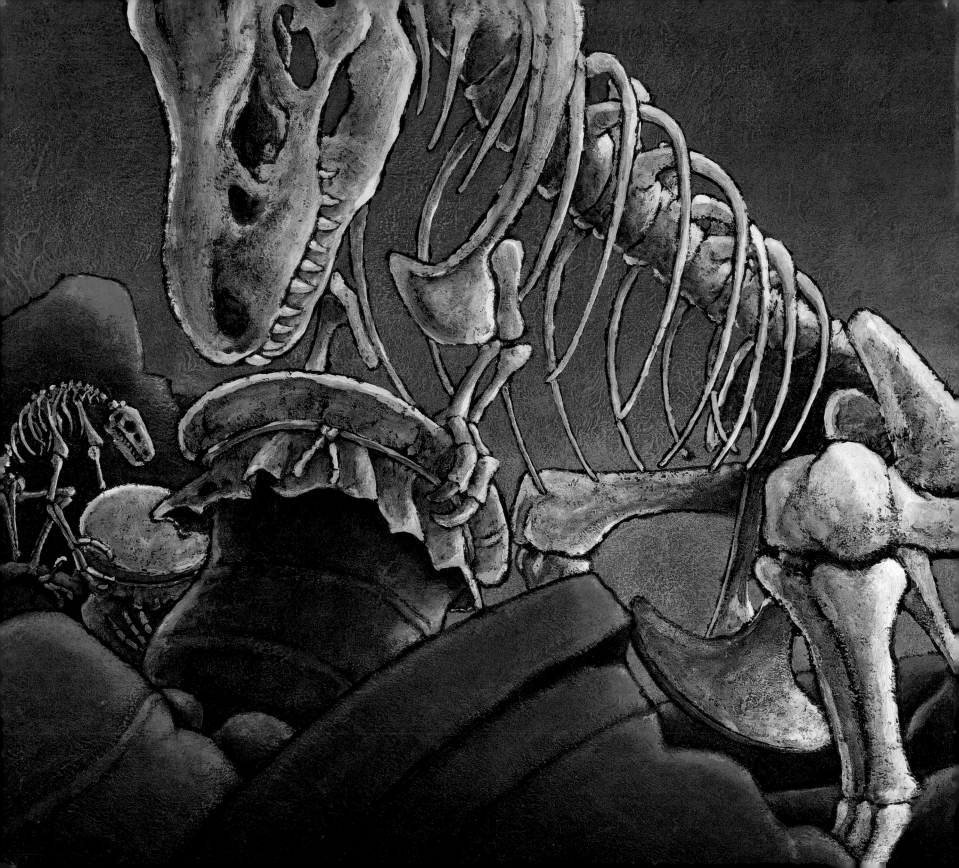

But when dark night gives way to the day, Drumheller dinosaurs stash drums away.

Then off they clatter through dinosaur land,

BOOMITY-BOOM RATTELY-CLACK

keeping the beat of their Drumheller band.

THUMPITY-THUMP WHICKETY-WHACK

Across the Badlands they creep to their beds,
unsnap tired bones and bury sleepy heads.

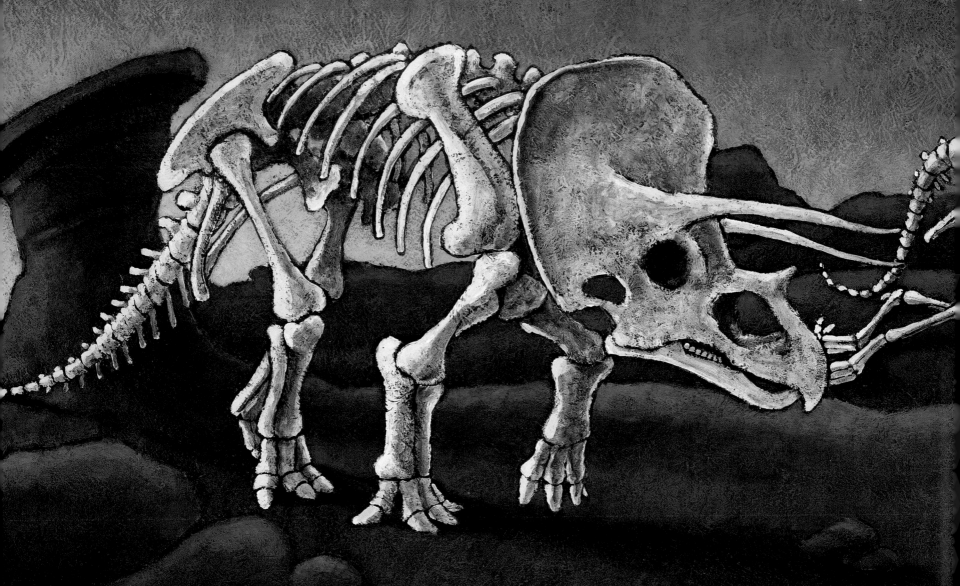

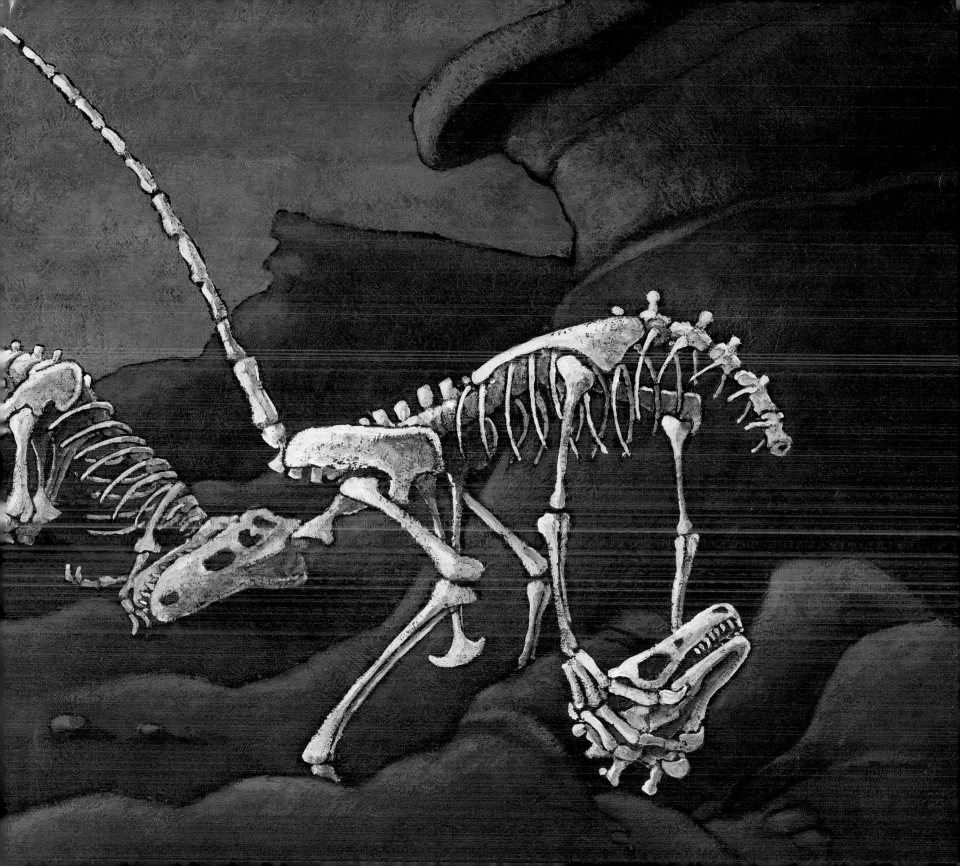

They're deep in the earth
by dawn's first light,

where they wait all day long
for dinosaur night.

To my five grandnieces, with love — R.H.

For Mia, who loves to dance on the wild side — B.S. & E.M.

Many thanks to the Royal Tyrrell Museum and Eric Snively, M.Sc., University of Calgary,
for their generous help in identifying the Drumheller dinosaurs.

Drumheller, Alberta, Canada, is one of the best places on Earth to find dinosaur bones, and it is
home to the world-famous Royal Tyrrell Museum. There are 350–400 known ancient dinosaur species in the
world, and over 60 are from Alberta! Some of these Drumheller dinosaurs are featured in this book.

Kids Can Press acknowledges the financial support of the Government of Ontario, through the Ontario
Media Development Corporation's Ontario Book Initiative; the Ontario Arts Council; the Canada Council
for the Arts; and the Government of Canada, through the BPIDP, for our publishing activity.

Published in Canada by	Published in the U.S. by
Kids Can Press Ltd.	Kids Can Press Ltd.
29 Birch Avenue	2250 Military Road
Toronto, ON M4V 1E2	Tonawanda, NY 14150

www.kidscanpress.com

The artwork in this book was rendered in acrylics, on gessoed paper.
The text is set in Spumoni and Alleycat.

Edited by Tara Walker
Designed by Bill Slavin and Esperança Melo
Printed and bound in Hong Kong, China, by Book Art Inc., Toronto

This book is smyth sewn casebound.

CM 04 0 9 8 7 6 5 4 3 2

National Library of Canada Cataloguing in Publication Data

Heidbreder, Robert
Drumheller dinosaur dance / written by Robert Heidbreder ; illustrated by Bill Slavin and Esperança Melo

ISBN 1-55337-393-6

I. Slavin, Bill II. Melo, Esperança III. Title.

PS8565.E42D78 2004   jC813'.54   C2003-906536-7

Kids Can Press is a *Corus*™ Entertainment company

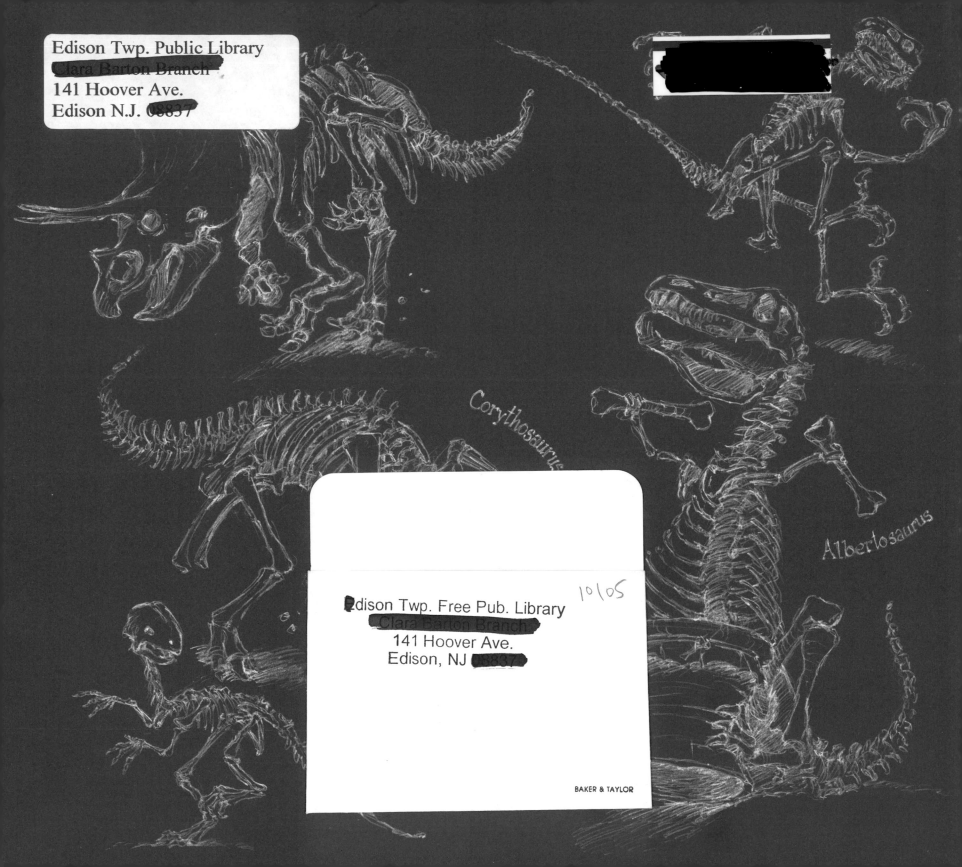

Corythosaurus

Albertosaurus